The Little Red Hen

Byron Barton

HarperCollins*Publishers*

The Little Red Hen Copyright © 1993 by Byron Barton Printed in the U.S.A. All rights reserved. Library of
Congress Cataloging-in-Publication Data The Little red hen / Byron Barton. p. cm. Summary: The little red hen
finds none of her lazy friends willing to help her plant, harvest, or grind wheat into flour, but all are eager to eat
the bread she makes from it. ISBN 0-06-021675-1. — ISBN 0-06-021676-X (lib. bdg.) [1. Folklore.] I. Barton,
Byron. PZ8.1.I.72Bar 1993 398.2—dc20 [E] 91-4051 CIP AC   1 2 3 4 5 6 7 8 9 10 First Edition

Once there were four friends—

a pig,   a duck,

a cat,

and a little red hen.

The little red hen had three baby chicks.

One day the little red hen was pecking in the ground,

and she found some seeds.

She went to her three friends and asked,
"Who will help me plant these seeds?"

"Not I," squealed the pig.
"Not I," quacked the duck.
"Not I," meowed the cat.

"Then I will plant the seeds," said the little red hen.
And she did.

And the seeds sprouted and grew into large stalks of wheat.

Then the little red hen asked her three friends,
"Who will help me cut these stalks of wheat?"

"Not I," meowed the cat.
"Not I," squealed the pig.
"Not I," quacked the duck.

"Then I will cut the wheat," said the little red hen.

And she did.

Then the little red hen asked her friends,
"Who will help me thresh this wheat?"

"Not I," squealed the pig.   "Not I," quacked the duck.

"Not I," meowed the cat.

"Then I will thresh the wheat," said the little red hen.

And she did.

Then the little red hen asked her friends,
"Who will help me grind these grains of wheat into flour?"

"Not I," squealed the pig.
"Not I," quacked the duck.
"Not I," meowed the cat.

"Then I will grind the wheat into flour," said the little red hen.

And she did.

Then the little red hen asked her three friends,
"Who will help me make this flour into bread?"

"Not I," meowed the cat.
"Not I," squealed the pig.
"Not I," quacked the duck.

"Then I will make the flour into bread," she said.

And she did.

Then the little red hen called to her friends,
"Who will help me eat   this bread?"

"I will," quacked the duck.
"I will," meowed the cat.
"I will," squealed the pig.

"Oh no," said the little red hen.

"We will eat the bread."

And they did—

the little red hen and her three little chicks.